SLIME TIME

By Jim and Jane O'Connor

Illustrated by Pat Porter

A STEPPING STONE BOOK

Random House New York

Text copyright © 1990 by Jim and Jane O'Connor. Illustrations copyright © 1990 by Pat Porter. All rights reserved under International and Pan-American Copyright Conventions. Published in the United States by Random House, Inc., New York, and simultaneously in Canada by Random House of Canada Limited, Toronto.

Library of Congress Cataloging-in-Publication Data
O'Connor, Jim. Slime time / by Jim and Jane O'Connor ; illustrated by Pat Porter. p. cm. "A Stepping Stone book." Summary: Danny and Jed become contestants on the children's television show "Slime Time," where wrong answers mean getting sprayed with whipped cream but right answers could lead to new skateboards. ISBN 0-679-90714-9 (lib. bdg.)— ISBN 0-679-80714-4 (pbk.) [1. Game shows—Fiction. 2. Television programs—Fiction.] I. O'Connor, Jane. II. Porter, Pat Grant, ill. III. Title. PZ7.02223S1 1990 [E]—dc20 89-77324 CIP AC

Manufactured in the United States of America   10 9 8 7 6 5 4 3 2 1

For Robby and Teddy

1

"Uh-oh! Something is weird in there," I told my best friend, Jed. We were standing in my room, staring at the door of my closet. My skateboard was inside. I was just about to pull open the door and grab it when I started to feel all cold and shivery. The hairs on the back of my neck tingled. And I was breaking out in goose bumps.

"I have a funny feeling I'm not going to like what I see," I told Jed.

"Ooh, Danny. I hate it when you get those feelings," Jed said nervously.

"That makes two of us," I said. You see, I am a real average kid—except for one thing.

Sometimes I can tell what's going to happen ahead of time. Like when Jed told me his mom was going to have a baby. Right away I knew it would be twins. Girl twins. And sure enough, Jed now has two little sisters named Donna and Dee Dee. I try not to think about this stuff too much. It gives me the creeps.

I went for the door. But Jed held my hand back. "Danny, what . . . what do you think is in there?" He looked scared.

I closed my eyes and concentrated. "I see creatures," I said slowly. "Strange tiny creatures in all different colors."

Jed's eyes bugged out. He picked up his skateboard and held it over his head, ready to clobber whatever was lurking in my closet.

Jed had come over so we could go skateboarding together in Central Park. We hadn't been on our boards for eight weeks—the whole time we were at Camp Tall Pines. We had just gotten home from camp last night. Now we could hardly wait to go zooming down Killer Hill.

I yanked the door open.

"Oh, no!" I yelled.

Jed jumped back.

"What? What?" he shouted. "What is it? A monster? An alien?"

I could only point. Jed peered over my shoulder. There was no alien or monster in my closet. There was only my skateboard,

right where I had left it two months ago. Only it sure didn't look the same. It used to be jet black with a Day-Glo green spider on it. Now it was painted a blotchy purple. And it was completely covered with stickers of chubby, rainbow-colored dinosaurs called Dinotots. Little kids were crazy about them. You couldn't turn on the television without seeing a Dinotots commercial. Disgusting!

"No offense. But that's the dorkiest skateboard I've ever seen," Jed said. "What kind of fiend would do something like that?"

Right on cue, my four-year-old brother, Patrick, appeared at the door of my room. He was clutching a blue Dinotot under his arm.

"Danny, Mommy says you and Jed have to take me to the playground."

I grabbed him. "You owe me a new skateboard!"

"I do not," he said. "You already got one. I made it nice for you while you were at camp." Patrick actually looked pleased with himself.

"You wrecked it!" I dragged Patrick and the skateboard into the living room where my mom was reading the newspaper. I held up the board so Mom could see it.

"Look! Look what he did." My voice was cracking, and my eyes started to tear up.

"Did you do that, Patrick?" my mother asked.

"No," Patrick said. He looked at Mom and gave her a big smile. "Daddy did it."

"Patrick, you know what I've told you about fibbing." Mom was making a feeble attempt to sound mad. That was typical. She thinks Patrick is a walking definition of the word *cute*. "Danny, I bet that paint will wash right off."

But it didn't. Jed and I spent an hour scrubbing it. The board stayed purple. I couldn't get the Dinotots stickers off either. They were stuck on with some kind of atomic glue. I was feeling more and more miserable.

"Hey! I know!" Jed's big round face lit up. "We hold a raffle. Twenty-five cents a ticket. Your board is the grand prize. I bet you'll make enough to buy a brand-new board!"

That's Jed for you. He's always thinking up

crazy ways to make money. I knew he was just trying to help, but I snapped back at him, "Grand prize? Get serious! This board isn't even booby-prize material."

We retreated into my room. Boy, did I feel rotten. There is nothing I like better than zooming down Killer Hill. There is a jump right in the middle where the pavement has buckled. You're only in the air for a second. But landing on your board and staying on is tough. It sure feels great when you hit it right! But no way could I go skateboarding now. I'd look like the biggest nerd in New York City.

"Come on, Danny. Try not to take it so hard," Jed said. "Maybe we can paint over your board tomorrow."

"It won't be the same." I let out a long sigh.

"Yeah, I know. I'd be pretty torn up too if I were you."

We both kicked off our sneakers and flopped on my bed. Some homecoming this was.

Jed looked at the clock. "It's four thirty. Almost time for dinner."

I had to smile. If Jed's mind isn't on money, it's on food. At camp when they asked us our favorite sport, Jed said forklifting!

"*Slime Time* should be starting soon. Want to watch?" I asked.

"Sure," Jed said, so I flicked on the tube. A commercial for Dinotots was ending.

"*Aieee!*" I screamed like I was being tortured. "Not Dinotots!" I covered my eyes so I wouldn't have to watch the army of Dinotots stomping their way through a pretend swamp. Unfortunately, I could still hear the stupid Dinotots jingle.

"Dinotots, tough and small.
Don't get one, collect them all!
Dinotots—only from Major Toys."

The commercial was over. And a second later I heard a voice yelling, "What time is it, kids?"

I opened my eyes to see the King of Goo, Marv Ballou, running through the studio audience while all the kids yelled back at him, "It's SLIME TIME!"

Slime Time is our favorite TV show. We hadn't seen it once while we were at camp.

On the show, kids answer questions and get slimed and gooped if they get them wrong. The kid who doesn't get slimed as much as the other one wins some neat stuff—like video games, cassettes, BMX bikes, and trips to places like Disney World.

First Marv Ballou introduced the two contestants, Jason and Kimberly. Then the questions started. Right away Jason missed one and got a bunch of raw eggs cracked on his head. Worse yet, he was loving it!

Then Kimberly's turn came. You could tell she was smart. She either got the answers right or she let Jason try for the hard ones. He missed every time. Then they would throw a chocolate pie in his face or spray him with whipped cream. Once he had to dive into a little wading pool of lemon Jell-O. And he kept grinning away.

"Boy, I never saw anyone get zero before," Jed said. "I bet even I could do better than that."

By the end of the show Kimberly had won, 180 points to nothing. Marv Ballou gave Jason the home version of *Slime Time*. It's what all the losers get. Then Marv put his arm around Kimberly.

"Kimberly," he said as the *Slime Time* theme song played, "you have won a Quest for Blooper video game; a trip to our nation's capital, Washington, D.C.; an official Wally Wallbanger Pro-Am skateboard . . ."

Marv Ballou went on to announce all the other great prizes that Kimberly had won. But all I could think about was that Wally Wallbanger Pro-Am skateboard. It had double rockers, mag trucks, a Day-Glo orange flaming skull, and Wally Wallbanger's name on it. It was the board of my dreams. I had seen one advertised in *Skateboard Maniac* magazine. It cost a fortune.

"Awesome," I said. "If only there were some way for me to get on *Slime Time,* I just know there's a Wally Wallbanger board out there with my name on it."

"Actually, Danny, they've got Wally's name on them."

Sometimes Jed can be kind of thick. I threw one of his sneakers at him.

"No! I mean one of those boards should be mine!" I turned off the tube and turned back to Jed. "Look. I can't go skateboarding until I get a new board. Patrick doesn't have any money. I'm broke. And my parents are going to say my old board is okay even though it looks like a girl's. Winning a Wally Wallbanger on *Slime Time* is my only hope."

Jed yawned and pulled on his sneakers. It was time for him to go home.

"Well, I bet you would do great on *Slime Time*," he said, tucking his skateboard under his arm. "You'd probably ace all the questions with your ESP."

It really bugs me when Jed says stuff like that. "I've told you a million times," I said. "It doesn't work that way."

"You knew about the Dinotots on your board

before you opened the closet. I'm a witness."

"I only had a feeling about little creatures," I said as I walked Jed to the front door of our apartment. "Not Dinotots. And I had no idea about the skateboard. Besides, I never know when I'm going to get one of those feelings. If I was on *Slime Time,* I'd have to win with my brains alone."

The elevator came and Jed got in. As the doors closed I stole an envious look at his board.

I had a feeling—not one of my strange feelings, just a plain old bad feeling—that it was going to be a long time before I was on wheels again.

2

When I woke up the next morning, the first thing I saw was my skateboard. I swear it had gotten uglier overnight. I shoved it under my bed so I wouldn't have to look at it. I was in some rotten mood. And it didn't get any better when Mom told me I had to go to the dentist at noon. After all the candy I'd eaten at camp, I probably needed a whole set of false teeth!

I was digging into a bowl of cereal and trying to ignore Patrick when the doorbell rang.

It was Jed.

His face was bright red. Sweat dripped from his forehead. And there was a crazy gleam in his eyes. There's only one thing that gets Jed so worked up. Money.

"Came as fast as I could . . ." he huffed. "Not going to believe this. . . ." Jed collapsed into a chair next to Patrick. He was waving a page torn out of the newspaper. "Our dream come true!"

I took the ripped page from Jed. In big black letters it said:

SLIME TIME GOES PRIME TIME

Twice the fun! Twice the goo! Twice the prizes!

Starting September 1st, America's hottest game show for kids will air at 7:30 each weekday evening on UBC/TV. Now kids can compete in teams of two for loads of fabulous prizes.

So if you are between the ages of nine and twelve, pick a partner in slime and come on down to the West Side Studios. Tryouts are today at three o'clock.

"Wow! Amazing!" I said.

"What does it say? Huh? Huh?" Patrick was tugging at my T-shirt. "Tell me-e-e-e!"

I pretended he was thin air.

"Do you think we should try out?" I asked Jed.

"What do you mean, *think*?" he cried. "Of course we're going to try out." Jed's chest had stopped heaving. The color in his face was back to normal. But he still had the crazy gleam in his eyes. "We are going to try out. We are going to get on *Slime Time*. And we are going to win!"

I wasn't so sure. I'm a pretty good student. I mean, we're not talking genius or anything. But Jed—well, even Jed admits that lunch is the only period where he really shines.

On the other hand, trying out for *Slime Time* did sound like a lot more fun than going to the dentist. So when Mom came out of the kitchen with a plate of bagels, I showed her the article. Right away I started begging and carrying on. "Please. Please. Please. This is the chance of a lifetime," I told her. "If I win, I could get a new skateboard. It would make up for the one Patrick wrecked. You've got to let me go!"

Mom looked doubtful. "Oh, I don't know, Danny. You're supposed to go to the dentist today. And I'm not crazy about that show. I saw it once. A little girl was rolled in egg and dipped in breadcrumbs. She ended up looking like a giant drumstick. I hate the idea of that happening to you."

"That stuff only háppens if you get the answers wrong," Jed said between bites of bagel.

I thought fast. "And—and if we got on the show, we would study real hard. We'd get all the answers right." I smiled at Mom. "It would be very educational."

I have to hand it to myself. *Educational* is a magic word with my mother. Mom looked uncertain. Then she sighed. "Well, I suppose I *could* change your dentist appointment."

Jed and I both punched the air with our fists. "All *right!*" we shouted. "We're going to be stars."

Jed thought we should think up a team name. "We'll write it on the backs of our T-shirts. It will make us stand out from all the other kids. Marv Ballou will love it."

"I know! I know! Call yourselves the Dinotots!" Patrick said.

We both made gagging noises.

"What about Double Trouble?" I said.

"Great! That's us. Double Trouble!"

Mom gave us two of my dad's old white T-shirts. Then we fished around in an art set of Patrick's for some markers and tubes of glitter. Jed is a pretty good artist. He printed out Double Trouble in thick green letters on the back of each T-shirt. Only he made the *B* in each word look like a bolt of lightning. We filled the lightning in with gold glitter. It took us forever, but they came out looking really cool.

By two thirty, we were in our T-shirts and ready to go. That's when Patrick threw a fit. All along he had figured he was coming with us.

"But this is for big boys only," my mom tried to explain. Patrick wasn't buying it. He stood perfectly still. He sucked in his breath until he turned as purple as my skateboard. Then he let out a scream. Boy, can that kid hold a note!

Jed and I headed for the front door. I felt bad for Mom. She was in for a long afternoon. But to tell the truth, I couldn't help smiling. For once, Patrick wasn't getting his way.

When we left, Patrick was parked in front of some dopey cartoon show, sobbing. But then a commercial for you-know-what came on. And, sure enough, it worked like a charm. Patrick stopped crying. While Jed and I waited for the elevator, we had to listen to that dumb Dinotots jingle again:

"Don't get one, collect them all!
Dinotots—only from Major Toys."

3

There were already loads of kids lined up in front of the West Side Studios by the time Jed and I got there.

"Rats!" Jed said, pointing to some kids ahead of us. It turned out we weren't the only ones who had thought up the T-shirt idea . . . or the name Double Trouble.

"It's okay," I told him. "Ours are much cooler than anybody else's."

"Just remember. Act peppy and smile a lot," Jed told me. "They go for that."

"Yeah. But personality won't get you on the show," the kid in front of us butted in. "They're going to ask a bunch of questions. And if you get more than one wrong, forget it. You're history." The kid told us his name was Howie and that he had skipped a grade. "My cousin is my teammate. She goes to a school for gifted children." Howie pointed to the tall girl beside him. She had a book called *1001 Useless Questions and Answers* and was studying all the kinds of stuff they ask on *Slime Time.* I sure wished I had thought of that.

Howie smiled at us. "I don't mean to brag. But I figure we're a sure thing to get on the show."

Jed got a nervous look on his face. But I just smiled right back at Howie. Because all of a sudden goose bumps were breaking out all over me. I was getting one of my feelings. One of my *strange* feelings. And I knew, as sure as Sunday comes after Saturday, that this Howie kid was not going to make it onto *Slime Time.* And Jed and I were!

Seconds later, the door to the studio opened, and a guy wearing a *Slime Time* T-shirt came out. He was carrying a clipboard and a megaphone. The line was really long now. There must have been two hundred kids on it. And every one of them started yelling and screaming when they saw the *Slime Time* guy.

"Quiet down, everybody. Now listen up," he yelled through the megaphone. "My name is Dave. I'm the talent scout for *Slime Time*. I want everyone to stand with their teammate. My assistant is going to take down your names. Then we'll call you inside to try out for the show."

By the time Dave's assistant had written down our names and addresses, the first team was already finished with their tryout. It was two girls wearing side ponytails.

"We made it! We made it!" the girls shouted as they came out the door. They were so happy they kept hugging each other and screaming.

But the next team that came out didn't look happy at all. They didn't say a word to anybody on the line. They just took off as fast as they could. Ditto for all the other teams ahead of us.

Jed was starting to look panicky.

"Take it easy, big guy," I said. "We're going to do fine. Trust me."

At that moment Howie and his cousin came out the studio door. They both looked like something out of a horror movie. Howie was real pale, and when he talked, he sounded like he was asleep.

"Unreal," he said. "We missed them all. Even ones I knew! After the first question, I just blanked out." He sounded like he still couldn't believe it. He kind of lurched away from us, like a zombie.

Jed was really sweating now. "Oh, Danny. We're sure to blow it." He swallowed hard. "Let's forget the whole thing and go home."

But Dave's assistant was already motioning to us. "Okay, you two. You're next."

I clamped my arm around Jed, and in we went.

4

The tryout was right in the studio where they tape *Slime Time*. A couple of huge TV cameras were pushed off to one side, and props were lying all around. There was a gigantic fake ice cream cone, the Jell-O wading pool, and lots of busted balloons.

"Hi, guys," said Dave. He was behind the stand that Marv Ballou uses on the show.

"HI, DAVE!" Jed yelled at the top of his lungs.

Dave smiled. I guess he could see Jed was kind of nervous. "Okay, you're Jed. And you're Danny, right?"

"RIGHT, DAVE!" Jed yelled again.

"Here's how it goes. I'm going to ask you ten questions. If you get nine out of ten right, you're on the show. But if you miss two questions, I'm afraid you're out. Ready?"

"READY, DAVE!" I yelled. Oh, no! Now I was doing it too.

"First question," Dave said, reading from a piece of paper. "Who was the Sultan of Swat?"

Easy!

"Babe Ruth!" I hollered.

"That's correct." Dave smiled. "Second question. What state is the Empire State?"

"New York!" I yelled again. Piece of cake! I grinned at Jed and gave him the thumbs-up sign.

"You're doing great so far," Dave told us. "But now the questions are going to get a little harder. So take your time. Talk over the answers if you want."

"Yeah, Danny," Jed whispered. He jabbed me with his elbow. "How about letting me answer one?"

"Ready," Dave said. "What is the largest river in the United States?"

"The Hudson!" Jed shouted before I could stop him. I groaned. What a lamebrain!

Dave shook his head. "I'm sorry. That's incorrect. Remember what I told you before. Talk it over."

"Airhead," I said, louder than I meant to. "The Mississippi is the largest. We learned that in third grade!"

Jed turned red. "I know that. I guess I got carried away."

"Well, don't get carried away," I said. "I want that skateboard. Just keep your mouth shut. Let me answer."

Jed turned redder. He was looking at Dave, who stood waiting to ask the next question.

And was I on a roll! I aced them all! I had

the answers as soon as Dave asked the questions.

"Congratulations!" Dave said at the end. He shook our hands. "You're going to be on *Slime Time*. Come back Saturday at five. That's when we'll tape the show."

"Yessss!" I yelled. "We made it!" I started hopping around doing a little victory dance as Jed headed for the door.

The second we were outside, kids swarmed around us.

"We got on the show!" I announced to the world. Kids started slapping me on the back and saying, "Way to go!"

Once I got past the mob of kids, I looked around for Jed. But he was nowhere in sight. Somehow we had lost each other in the crowd. So I ended up going home by myself.

Did I ever feel great! I was going to be on *Slime Time*. That skateboard was practically mine!

5

"Ta-da!" I shouted as I swung open the door to our apartment. "I have returned!"

Everybody was in the den. Mom was watching TV. Dad was reading a magazine with a can of soda in his hand. Patrick was under the coffee table. He was wearing the dinosaur costume Mom had bought him last Halloween, and he was growling.

"So how did it go?" Mom asked right away.

"Well," I said slowly, making the most of the moment. "We'll be on the show this Saturday!"

I had a feeling Mom was going to scream. She did.

Dad wasn't too cool either. He spit out a big mouthful of soda all over his shirt. Just like in a Three Stooges movie.

While Dad was coughing, Mom kept shrieking, "I can't believe it!" Then she went racing into their bedroom. "I'm calling your grandparents right now!"

Dad was right behind her. "I get the phone after you," I could hear Dad shouting. "My son! On TV!"

Now only Patrick and I were left in the den. Patrick stopped growling and poked his head up at me.

"Are you famous?"

"No. Not really," I said modestly.

Patrick looked disappointed and started growling again.

Mom came back to the den. "Grandma's line is busy. And so is your aunt Carol's. I'll try them again after Dad is off. Then I'll call your uncle Tim in Oregon. This is so exciting." Mom planted a big kiss on my forehead. "I bet Jed must be on cloud nine too."

Jed! I'd almost forgotten about him. As soon as Dad was finished calling all his relatives,

I dialed Jed's number. We sure had a lot of studying to do before Saturday.

Jed's mom answered the phone.

"Hold on. I'll get him," she told me. But a second later she got back on the line. "Sorry, Danny. I'm afraid Jed can't come to the phone now."

I waited fifteen minutes and called again.

"Hi," I said when I heard Jed's mother again. "Can Jed come to the phone now?"

Jed's mom put her hand over the phone. I could hear her arguing with Jed about something. At last Jed got on the line.

"What do you want?" he asked flatly.

"How about meeting at the library at ten o'clock tomorrow? We sure don't have much time before the show. I figure we could start studying sports stuff. Then maybe go on to history, and—"

"Gee, Danny. I didn't think *you* needed to study," Jed snapped. "*You* seemed to have all the answers already."

Whoa! Something was seriously wrong here.

"Jed. I don't get it. You sound mad. What's eating you?"

"You're such a genius," he said. "You figure it out."

I stopped. I thought about the tryout. Uh-oh. "Are you mad because I called you an airhead?" I asked uneasily.

"Bingo!"

"Well, that just p-p-popped out," I stammered. "But I got us on *Slime Time,* didn't I? Think about that!"

"Maybe so. But it was me who knew about the tryout, don't forget. And anyway," Jed went on, "I bet you only knew all that stuff because of your ESP."

"That's a big fat lie!" I started to say. But I never got the chance. Jed had already hung up on me.

Well, if that's how he wanted it, fine! I slammed down the phone too. Then I went into my room and practiced my TV smile in front of the mirror. Maybe I shouldn't have said what I did. But Jed didn't have to get so sore. He was going to be on TV. National TV. All because of me.

Every time the phone rang, I was sure it was going to be Jed calling to say he was stupid to get so mad. That's the way it usually works when we get into a fight. Either Jed or I will go, "Aw. This is dumb. Let's just forget it." And we do.

But Jed didn't call. "He's waiting for me to call *him*," I told myself.

Well, he better not hold his breath!

6

The next morning I got to the library as soon as it opened. I didn't budge until closing time. But did Jed ever show up? No! He was probably home watching reruns of *I Love Lucy* while I slaved away.

I sat at the last table in the main reading room with stacks of fact books in front of me. Boy, did I wind up knowing a lot! I knew that a man someplace in India had fingernails that were twelve inches long. I knew that a newborn kangaroo is so small it can fit in a teaspoon. I knew that *Connecticut* is spelled with only two *t*'s. And that the number one followed by a hundred zeros is called a *googol*.

Let me tell you, my brain got some work-out! By the time the library closed, my head felt like it was ready to burst from all the facts I was stuffing inside it.

I made it home just in time for *Slime Time*. I tried to see how many questions I could answer. Not to brag, but I was getting pretty good.

Then I started thinking about Jed. I knew he must be watching too. I looked over at my bulletin board. There was a picture tacked up of Jed and me at camp. We had our arms around each other. Jed was making donkey ears behind my head. I couldn't help feeling bad. Of all times to be in a fight!

Jed never called that night. And the next day I made a point to walk by his house on my way to the library. I was hoping we'd run into each other. I pictured how we'd sock each other in the arm and be friends again. Poof! Like magic. But it didn't happen. And I spent the whole day studying by myself.

Once I got home and *Slime Time* was over, there was nothing to do. All my other friends were still away for the summer. I tried reading a book from our school reading list. Then I played Dinotots with Patrick for a while. That shows how desperate I was!

Patrick took the nice new blue one. I got stuck with an old orange one that had melted spikes from the time Patrick tried cooking it in the oven.

"Me hungry! Me eat you!" Patrick roared, marching his Dinotot over to me.

"Aargh!" I screamed. "You got me!" I flipped my Dinotot over on its back. There were half-melted letters spelling out MAJOR TOYS on its belly.

Just then Mom poked her head into my room.

"I thought I heard you two playing." She looked like she wanted to grab a video cam to remember the moment. But Mom is no dummy. She knows I think playing with Patrick is about as much fun as getting a nosebleed. That evening she asked me how come Jed wasn't around.

"I thought you two would be spending every waking moment together," she said. "You know. Quizzing each other for the show?"

"No," I said. "Uh . . . we decided to study alone. That way we won't be going over the same stuff." I pretended to go back to the book I was reading. It was called *1000 Most Misspelled Words*. I caught Mom and Dad exchanging looks. They knew something was wrong. But they didn't push it.

That night I had a dream about Jed and me. We were on *Slime Time*. The girls on the other team—they were named Fawn and Linda—were covered with slime. We were too. The dream was so real, I could feel chocolate sauce dripping down my neck. It was time for the last question. That was going to decide the winner.

Marv Ballou cleared his throat. "Here it comes. Think carefully before you answer. The final question is . . ."

Marv Ballou kept on speaking. But I couldn't hear a word. It was like watching television with the sound turned off. I felt completely frozen. It was the last question, and I didn't know the answer.

I woke up with a start. Sweat, not chocolate sauce, was dripping down my neck. My heart was going double time. I was having one of my strange feelings again. I knew that dream was telling me something. Jed and I were going to lose. Good-bye, Wally Wallbanger skateboard. Hello, home version of *Slime Time*!

7

The next day the library stayed open late. I spent nine long hours there. I figured if I could learn enough, then maybe the dream would not come true. Maybe there was still a chance I could win.

That night I was scared to go to sleep. I knew—don't ask me how—I just knew the dream was going to come back. There's a glow-in-the-dark poster of the stars taped on the ceiling over my bed. I tried to stay awake by picking out the constellations. First I found the Big Dipper, then the Crab, then . . .

Before I knew it, I was asleep and back in TV-land. The dream was just like the first one—Jed and I against the two girls, down to the last question.

Once again Marv Ballou's lips started moving, only no sound came out. Then something really weird happened. A door opened in Marv Ballou's podium and out stepped Patrick! He was dressed in a little blazer and bow tie. Just like Marv Ballou.

"Airhead!" Patrick said to me in a mean voice. "You are so dumb! This is all you need." Then he shoved one of his Dinotots into my hand.

I woke up feeling mad at Patrick and more confused than ever. What did it all mean? Was Patrick giving me some kind of clue? I didn't have much time to find out.

The next morning I headed straight for the dinosaur shelf at the library. The last question had to be about dinosaurs. What else could the dream mean? I started with *Apatosaurus* and went all the way to *Zephyrosaurus*. Meat eaters. Plant eaters. Dinosaurs as small as chickens. Dinosaurs as tall as houses. I read about them all.

I left the library feeling better. No matter what the last question on *Slime Time* was going to be, I was pretty sure I had the answer.

On the way home I walked by the park. I passed Killer Hill. I closed my eyes and pictured myself on a brand-new Wally Wallbanger doing *S* curves all the way down it.

But the picture was missing something. Or somebody, I should say. All of a sudden I thought about the tryout again, and this time I got a sick feeling in my stomach. I remembered the nervous look Jed gets whenever a test is handed back. And how he always gets stuck in the lowest reading group. I was really feeling bad now. How could I have said that stuff? What kind of friend was I?

When I got home, I knew what I had to do. It took me a while to work up my nerve. But right after dinner I picked up the phone. I dialed Jed's number.

One ring. Two rings. Three rings.

"Hello," said a squeaky little girl's voice. "We are sorry we are not home right now."

Rats! It was Donna or Dee Dee, I never knew which, on the answering machine.

"Please leave a message after the beep."

I swallowed hard.

"Jed. It's me. Danny. I'm calling to wish you good luck—I mean *us*—good luck tomorrow. And—um—Jed." I stopped for a moment. I could just picture Jed's mom or dad listening to this message. I went on anyway. "I know I can be a big jerk sometimes. And I'm really sorry for how I acted at the tryout. Win or lose, I hope we're still friends."

There. I had said it. I went to bed feeling better. But that didn't last long. The dream came back again! It ended just like before, with Patrick handing me that dumb Dinotot. And me blowing the last question.

I woke up sure of one thing. Jed and I were doomed. We were heading for disaster. We were going to get demolished. Devastated. Destroyed. We were dead. And the show hadn't even begun!

8

"Time to go!"

There they were. The three words I'd been afraid of hearing all day.

"Coming, Mom," I croaked. My throat felt as dry as the Sahara, which, I now knew, is the largest desert in the world.

Downstairs we all piled into a cab—Mom, Dad, Patrick, and me. I was wearing jeans and my Double Trouble T-shirt. Mom and Dad were all dressed up like they were going to a party. Patrick looked like he always does—a total mess.

The cab pulled up to the curb, and a minute later we were walking inside the West Side Studios.

The place seemed huge—even bigger than it had looked at the tryout. There were rows and rows of empty red seats. I could see Jed's parents and the twins—but no Jed—down in the very front row. Onstage a man was putting two big cards that said JED and DANNY on one desk. I looked over at the other desk. Sure enough, the cards said FAWN and LINDA. Just like in my dream!

Mom and Dad hugged me and wished me good luck. Patrick waved as a guy came and led me backstage.

"Your teammate is already here," the guy told me. "He said he ate an entire sausage pizza right before he came over." The guy laughed. "Most kids are too nervous to eat anything. How do you feel?"

"Like most kids," I said. By now I didn't have a single nail left to bite. I was sweating buckets. And I had to go to the bathroom. I was definitely, positively, one hundred percent very, very nervous.

The guy led me into a little room backstage. Right away I saw Jed. He was standing by a big mirror turning his head from side
to side. He had on his Double Trouble T-shirt
too. I was really scared he was still mad at
me. But when he saw me, Jed smiled.

"Yo, Danny!" he said. "Which side do you
think is my best side for the camera?"

I smiled for the first time that day. I went
up and gave Jed a big high-five. "You got my
message?"

"Yeah." Jed gave me a high-five back. That
was all it took. Jed and me, we don't like to
talk a lot about serious stuff. But I knew we
were friends again.

"I'm feeling real good about today," Jed said.
He was bouncing around on his feet, the way
boxers do before a big fight. "Hey, maybe I
have some ESP too. Because I know we're
going to win. And win BIG." Jed socked me
in the arm.

I managed a weak smile. "Sure, Jed."

By five minutes to five, we were seated at
our desk. Fawn and Linda, who wore T-shirts
that said SLIME SISTERS, were across from us.

Each team had a box with a red button on it. We were supposed to hit the button as soon as we knew the answer.

The studio was packed. The lights on the set were real bright. But when I squinted I could make out Mom and Dad—Patrick too—waving like crazy. The music to *Slime Time* started. A guy shouted, "Five seconds to showtime!" And then the King of Goo, Marv Ballou himself, appeared under a spotlight.

"What time is it, everybody?" he yelled into his microphone.

"Slime Time!" the studio audience yelled back.

This was it! Just like I'd seen so many times on TV. Only now it was me—ME!—up on stage.

Marv introduced all of us to the studio audience. Then he cleared his throat and said in a serious voice, "Okay, teams. You know the rules. Listen to each question. The first team to hit the button gets to try and answer. If you miss, you get slimed, and the other team gets the question. If they miss, it's Slime Time for them, too.

"Ready? This one is for ten points. Good luck." Marv paused. Then he said, "Name the last president born and raised in the Lone Star State."

I heard the buzzer go off. Holy guacamole! It was me who pushed it!

"All right, Double Trouble. For ten points, who was the last president born and raised in the Lone Star State?"

"Lyndon Baines Johnson," I answered.

"Correct! And Double Trouble scores ten points!"

"Way to go!" Jed slapped me on the back. But we had to shut up. Marv was already on the next question.

"If *Mississippi* has two *p*'s, four *i*'s, and four *s*'s, how many *n*'s and *t*'s are in *Connecticut*?"

I knew that too! I lunged for the buzzer.

But Jed beat me to it. "Two *n*'s and three *t*'s!" he shouted. I wanted to groan. But I caught myself.

Marv shook his head sadly. "I'm sorry. That's incorrect. And that means . . . IT'S SLIME TIME!"

The gold curtains behind Marv opened to

reveal something called the Big Mouth. I'd seen it on TV before. But it looked much worse in real life. You have to crawl through a pair of giant rubber lips, then slide down a long "tongue" into a pool of chocolate sauce.

"Okay, boys. Down you go!" Marv said.

Jed went first. He climbed through the lips and whooshed down the slide, sending up a wave of chocolate sauce when he hit the pool. He came up with a big smile, licking his lips. The audience loved it.

I went second. I held my nose and closed my eyes. I thought there would be a splash. But there wasn't. Chocolate sauce is a whole lot thicker than water. When I hit, it felt like being sucked down into chocolate quicksand.

I had a hard time scrambling out, but I made it.

"Danny, I'm real sorry I messed up," Jed said as we returned to our seats, leaving a trail of chocolate.

"No sweat," I said. I wiped my face with the towel Marv handed me. "I didn't know the answer either." I figure there are times when a white lie comes in handy.

The Slime Sisters got the Connecticut question right. But they goofed up on a multiplication problem. So they had to sit in a little convertible with the top down and go through a car wash that sprayed whipped cream all over them.

Next, I messed up. I said there were eight quarts in a gallon instead of four. I could have kicked myself. This time, Jed and I had to have a pillow fight with two pillows that were

bigger than we were. The second we started
swatting at each other, the pillows tore open.
Millions of little yellow feathers flew out. The
feathers stuck to all the chocolate sauce, so
Jed and I ended up looking like Big Bird on
a bad day.

After that we went along for a while with
no misses. We'd get an answer. The Slime
Sisters would get one. Jed knew that a famous dessert named after a state was called
a baked alaska. I got the five colors of the
Olympics symbol—black, red, yellow, blue,
and green.

The questions came faster and faster. I forgot all about the audience, the hot lights, how messy we were, even that we were on TV. All I could see was Marv Ballou and the red button in front of me.

It was almost the end of the show. The score was tied, 70–70. But that was no surprise to me.

"Okay, Slime Sisters and Double Trouble," Marv said. "Here it is. The tiebreaker. Whichever team answers correctly is going to win some fabulous *Slime Time* prizes."

Jed looked at me and went thumbs up.

My heart was beating so hard it felt like my whole body was shaking.

"Name the world's largest toy company," Marv said slowly. "Makers of Burpsy Betsy dolls, Little Generals action figures . . . and Dinotots."

Yikes! Now I understood what my dream was telling me. Frantically I tried to think how that dumb jingle went. I couldn't remember. I squeezed my eyes shut. I tried to picture the melted letters on that Dinotot's belly. No luck. I felt sick. Not only was I going to lose the game. I was going to lose my lunch on national television!

The buzzer went off.

"Okay, Double Trouble," Marv said. "Your question."

Our question?

"I know it, Danny!" Jed whispered. "Trust me on this one." Then he turned to Marv Ballou.

"It's Major Toys!" he shouted.

Marv was nodding yes. The audience started cheering. Jed threw himself on me—all 103 pounds of him. I just sat there with a dumb grin on my face, covered with chocolate and feathers. My dream hadn't been wrong. It had just stopped too soon. *I* hadn't known the answer. But Jed had. And we had won!

After that a lot of stuff happened all at once. I remember the applause sign flashing and Patrick running up onstage and Jed raising his hands over his head like Rocky.

I could see my mom and dad. They were hugging each other and screaming. Every once in a while my dad would put two fingers in his mouth and give a big screeching whistle.

By the time the clapping died down, the Slime Sisters had disappeared with their home versions of *Slime Time*. Then Marv Ballou announced all the prizes we'd won.

"Jed and Danny," Marv said, smiling into the camera. "You have each won seventy dollars in cash, five video games of your choice, a year's free pass to Scream-o-rama Fun Park, a three-inch color TV, and the superdeluxe Wally Wallbanger Pro-Am skateboard."

Yes! He had said it! And I wasn't dreaming!

After that the *Slime Time* theme song started playing. Marv pretended to put his arms around our shoulders. But he didn't really touch us. I guess the chocolate syrup and feathers grossed him out.

"Boy, did we clean up!" I told Jed over the applause. "And I've got you to thank for all this."

"Nah. We did it together," Jed said. "I can't wait to get out of here and try our new Wallys!"

And that's exactly what we did. Jed and I hit the park that afternoon. My Wally Wallbanger was really a beaut. Right down to the flaming skull on the deck. Jed's was the same as mine. Only his wheels were green, and mine were red. Awesome!

I was feeling so good that I even let Patrick tag along. After all, he has his own board now. It's purple, and it's covered with stickers of Dinotots.

About the Authors

"I love to watch game shows, and I've always wanted to be on one," says JIM O'CONNOR. "You get to be on national television, and if you win, there's always a great prize, like a skateboard!"

JANE O'CONNOR says, "When we were writing *Slime Time,* we just wanted to gross kids out. I hope it worked!"

Jim and Jane O'Connor are the authors of *The Ghost in Tent 19,* a 1988 Stepping Stone. They live in New York City with their two sons.

About the Illustrator

PAT PORTER was three years old when she did her first illustration on the wallpaper behind her father's armchair. Since becoming a grownup, she has illustrated 21 books. And of all the books she's illustrated, she says that *Slime Time* is by far the most intriguing story.

She lives and works in New York City.